Dear Parents,

Welcome to the Scholastic Reader series. We have taken over 80 years of experience with teachers, parents, and children and put it into a program that is designed to match your child's interests and skills.

Level 1—Short sentences and stories made up of words kids can sound out using their phonics skills and words that are important to remember.

Level 2—Longer sentences and stories with words kids need to know and new "big" words that they will want to know.

Level 3—From sentences to paragraphs to longer stories, these books have large "chunks" of texts and are made up of a rich vocabulary.

Level 4—First chapter books with more words and fewer pictures.

It is important that children learn to read well enough to succeed in school and beyond. Here are ideas for reading this book with your child:

- Look at the book together. Encourage your child to read the title and make a prediction about the story.
- Read the book together. Encourage your child to sound out words when appropriate. When your child struggles, you can help by providing the word.
- Encourage your child to retell the story. This is a great way to check for comprehension.
- Have your child take the fluency test on the last page to check progress.

Scholastic Readers are designed to support your child's efforts to learn how to read at every age and every stage. Enjoy helping your child learn to read and love to read.

—Francie Alexander
Chief Education Officer
Scholastic Education

D0283364

No part of this publication may be reproduced, or stored in a retrieval system, or transmitted in any form or by any means, electronic, mechanical, photocopying, recording, or otherwise, without written permission of the publisher. For information regarding permission, write to Scholastic Inc., Attention: Permissions Department, 557 Broadway, New York, NY 10012.

Copyright © 2005 by DC Comics.
Batman and all related characters and elements
are trademarks of and © DC Comics.
All rights reserved. Published by Scholastic Inc.
SCHOLASTIC, CARTWHEEL BOOKS, and associated logos are
trademarks and/or registered trademarks of Scholastic Inc.

Library of Congress Cataloging-in-Publication data.

Ciencin, Scott.
Batman : green Gotham / by Scott Ciencin ; illustrated by Rick Burchett.
p. cm. -- (Scholastic reader. Level 3)
"Cartwheel books."
"Batman created by Bob Kane."
Summary: When Poison Ivy tries to turn Gotham City into a jungle, Batman comes to the rescue.
ISBN 0-439-47102-8 (pbk.)
[1. Heroes--Fiction. 2. Plants--Fiction. 3. Mystery and detective stories.] I. Burchett, Rick, ill. II. Title. III. Series.
PZ7.C4907Bat 2005

[Fic]--dc22   2005005659

10 9 8 7 6 5 4 3 2 1   05 06 07 08 09
Printed in the U.S.A. 23 • First printing, September 2005

BATMAN™

GREEN GOTHAM

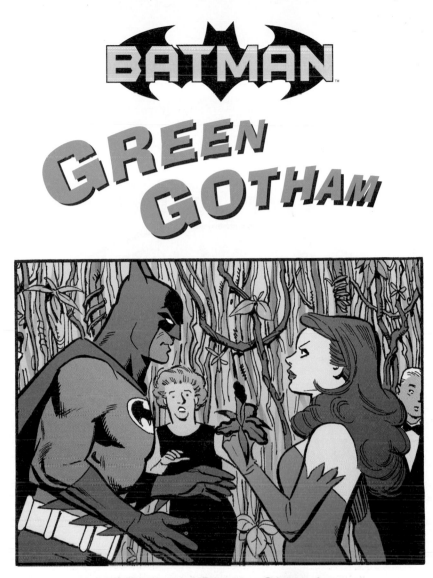

Written by **Scott Ciencin**

Illustrated by **Rick Burchett**

Batman created by Bob Kane

Scholastic Reader — Level 3

Cartwheel ®
·B·O·O·K·S·

SCHOLASTIC INC.

New York Toronto London Auckland Sydney
Mexico City New Delhi Hong Kong Buenos Aires

CANCEL

WASECA-LESUEUR REGIONAL LIBRARY

CHAPTER ONE

PLANT POWER

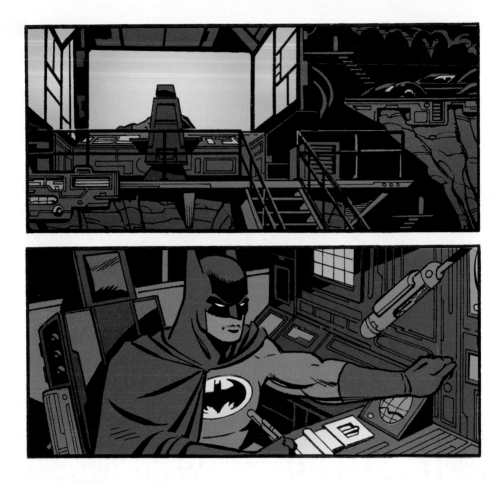

Bruce Wayne was one of the richest men in Gotham City. He lived in Wayne Manor, above a secret cave — the Batcave!

That's because Bruce was also Batman!

Every evening, Batman carefully checked his crime-fighting tools and equipment. Then he would go out on patrol.

There was a party at the Gotham City
Botanical Gardens. Everyone in Gotham
City was there. The Pink Orchid, a very rare
flower, was in a special show. People were

dressed in black from head to toe. Black climbing roses with sharp thorns and other plants covered the walls.

Late into the night, everyone was surprised by a loud crash.

A tall woman with flaming red hair broke open the case holding the Pink Orchid and grabbed the flower. She ran for the door. But before she could get away, a window flew open high above. A dark shape fell to the ground. A cape opened up like the wings of a bat.

"Why, Batman," Ivy said. "So nice to see you!"

"I wish I could say the same, Poison Ivy!" said Batman.

Ivy waved her hand at the plants in the room. Suddenly, the roses snapped at the scared guests. Long vines crawled toward people as they ran for the exits. The plants curled around people's legs and bodies and would not let them move.

Ivy ran toward the back door. Batman wanted to run after her, but he knew lives were in danger. He sighed as the door closed behind her, and he began to help people break free from the plants.

Batman knew wherever Poison Ivy had gone, she was probably up to no good.

Poison Ivy was once Pamela Isley, a brilliant student of plants. But one day, an experiment went wrong and made her body more plantlike than human. She gained the power to control nature with her mind. She could also give off natural smells that hypnotized people.

Since the accident, all Poison Ivy cared about was plant life and nature. She wanted nothing to do with people. She would not be happy until the world was overcome by plants.

Poison Ivy might have escaped this time. But Batman knew he would not have long to wait before she showed up again.

CHAPTER TWO

RARE ROOT ROBBERY

A NICE, QUIET MORNING, UNTIL...

Two days later, Bruce Wayne sat down to breakfast in the dining room of Wayne Manor. His butler, Alfred, carried in a tray with a plate of eggs, bacon, toast, and a glass of orange juice. Next to that was a copy of the *Gotham City Gazette*.

"Good morning, Master Bruce," Alfred said.

"Good morning, Alfred," Bruce said. "Anything interesting in the newspaper today?"

"Yes, there is, sir," Alfred said, placing the

tray in front of Bruce. "Look at page twenty."

As he sipped his juice, Bruce turned to the page.

"Do you think this is Poison Ivy's doing, sir?" asked Alfred.

SECOND PLANT STORE ROBBED!

Over the past two days, two plant stores have been robbed. No money has been taken— only rare roots and herbs. The clerks could not remember anything about the person who had held them up.

Bruce pushed back his chair and stood up. "Of course. The question is, what's she up to?" he said. He rushed out of the room, leaving Alfred, and his breakfast, behind.

CHAPTER THREE

SOMETHING STINKS

Nature's Grocery was a small store on
a quiet street in Gotham City. Inside, there
were beautiful plants and bottles of natural
medicines and herbs for sale.

Just before lunch, a beautiful red-haired woman walked into the store. She was wearing green pants and a green coat.

"May I help you?" Herbert asked. He sniffed the air. His store usually smelled nice, like flowers and herbs. But there was something else in the air. Something that made his head spin. The smell got stronger when the woman leaned over the counter.

"Yes, you may," she said.

Herbert took a deep breath. He felt as though his head was swimming.

YES, YOU MAY.

"Please fill this order for me," she said and handed Herbert a piece of paper. On it was a list of different rare herbs and roots.

Herbert put everything together in a big box. He handed it to the woman.

"Is there anything else I can do for you?" he asked.

She smiled sweetly. "Yes. Forget everything about me after I've left!"

Herbert blinked his eyes as she left the store. He stared out the window. He could not remember a thing the woman had bought.

HUH?

CHAPTER FOUR

HIS HANDS ARE TIED

The woman in green stepped outside
Nature's Grocery. She held her box of stolen
goods under her arm.

"Nice day for shopping, isn't it, Poison Ivy?"

Batman stepped out from the shadows.

"It is," Poison Ivy agreed. "I really would
hate for you to spoil it."

Batman pointed to the box she was holding.
"I wouldn't have to . . . if you had just paid."

Ivy smiled. "Pay for my pretty plants?
That would be like paying for the air I
breathe."

"But you will pay for your crimes,"
said the Dark Knight. "I'll have you put in
Arkham Asylum, Ivy."

"Maybe," she said, "but not quite *yet*!"

Suddenly, Batman heard the sound of
breaking glass. The branches of the plants
in Nature's Grocery were growing very fast.
They broke through the store window and
wrapped themselves around Batman!

THW'PPP!

BATMAN WAS IN TROUBLE!

Batman fought with the branches, but there were too many. They held his chest, his arms, and his legs and lifted him off the ground. He couldn't breathe!

"I'd love to stay and watch," Ivy said. "But I'm late for a very important date. Good-bye, Batman!"

With a brief wave, Poison Ivy walked away.

One branch closed around Batman's neck. Batman pulled with all his strength on another branch holding his right arm. If only he could reach his Utility Belt!

The branches tightened around his neck and chest. Inch by inch, Batman's fingers moved toward his belt.

Just as he thought he would pass out, his finger pushed a hidden button on his belt. A cloud of mist shot from a small hole.

As soon as the mist touched the plants,

Batman felt the branches let go. Soon they returned to normal size.

Batman raced to where he had left the Batmobile. But something was different. A huge tree the size of a skyscraper was blocking his door. It had not been there before. Batman had no idea where the tree had come from. He climbed in the other door, sat behind the wheel, and sped away.

CHAPTER FIVE

WEIRD SCIENCE

Batman's next stop was back to the Gotham City Botanical Gardens.

William Holt was in charge of the Botanical Gardens. He knew everything about plants. When he wasn't looking for rare plants to show in his gardens, he was reading everything he could about the plant world.

Batman arrived to find William reading a book about rare roots and herbs. He was smiling.

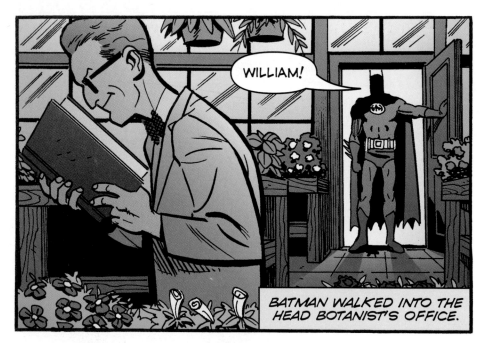

WILLIAM!

BATMAN WALKED INTO THE HEAD BOTANIST'S OFFICE.

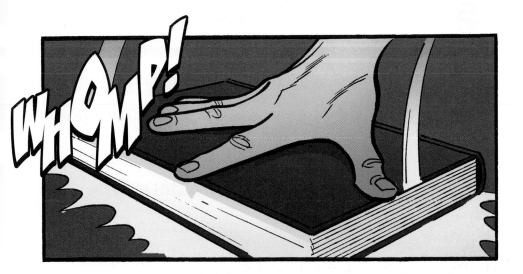

"William!" Batman said.

"Batman! Hello!" William quickly closed his book. "How may I help you?"

"I'm looking for a reason why Poison Ivy would have taken the Pink Orchid," Batman said. "Everyone in the plant world knows she took it, so she can't sell it. And you are the only man who would know why she did it."

William stared at Batman. "Poison Ivy probably took it because she is the only one who could see its rare beauty. She is the only one in this town with a *true* love of flowers!"

A loud alarm rang through the building. It was time to water the gardens. William picked up a watering can and stood up. "Are we finished here?"

"No, William—not just yet." Batman looked down and quickly opened the book on William's desk. There was a piece of paper marking one part. Batman read the title:

Pink Orchid's Pollen Combines with Rare Herbs to Heal Sick Youth

William saw Batman reading the book and smiled.

Batman thought for a second, then he knew where he should go. He rushed toward the door. He knew he almost had Poison Ivy.

William put down his watering can. "Wait, Batman! Poison Ivy means no harm! Please don't hurt her!" But Batman did not see him laughing secretly.

The Dark Knight jumped in his Batmobile and raced downtown. Trees bigger than office buildings and flowers as big as lampposts blocked the roads. Something strange was going on in Gotham City.

HUGE TREES WERE GROWING EVERYWHERE!

CHAPTER SIX

TREEHOUSE TRICKS

Batman was on his way to Gotham City
Hospital. He thought that maybe, this time,
Poison Ivy was using her power over plants
for good.

But before he got there, Batman saw
something strange outside the Batmobile's
window. All of the trees and plants along the
side of the road were growing really fast!
They grew taller and taller every second.
Their roots moved along the streets, making
it hard for cars to drive.

Batman looked into the distance. One tree stood even higher than the rest. Its leaves were so far up that Batman could barely see them in the sky.

Batman sped toward the tree.

Later, Batman pulled up in front of Gotham City Park. He ran to the huge tree in the center of the park.

The tree was hollow. Inside, Ivy was holding the Pink Orchid in one hand. With her other hand, she removed the pollen from the flower's center. She mixed the pollen with the herbs she had stolen from Nature's Grocery.

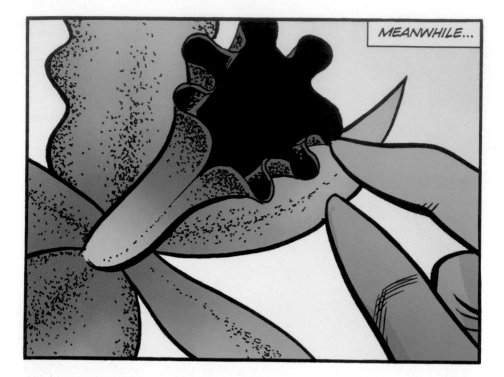

MEANWHILE...

Next to her stood William Holt. He held a large plastic container filled with gallons of dirt. Ivy sprinkled the mixture in the dirt.

"See, William, it's so easy," she said. "First I will turn Gotham City into Gotham Forest. Then our plants will take over the world! We will be the only humans on Earth!"

William laughed. "Only we will have the potion to stop the plants," he said. "And with

Batman off our track, our plan will be easier than ever!"

Batman stepped out of the shadows.

"Not so fast, Ivy!"

He ran toward Ivy and William. But they didn't move. They knew as soon as Batman came close, Poison Ivy's smells would stop him.

"Batman, even *you* can't stop the power of my plants!" she yelled.

But Batman didn't slow down! Then Ivy saw the clear mask he wore over his mouth and nose. He couldn't smell her! He had protected himself from her tricks!

William and Ivy froze with shock. Batman grabbed Poison Ivy with one hand and William with the other. He handcuffed them together. Then he took the potion.

BATMAN'S MASK SAVES HIM!

"Don't worry, Ivy," said Batman. "Where you're going, you won't be around humans for a long time."

Batman and Commissioner Gordon stood outside Poison Ivy's cell at Arkham Asylum. Her cell looked like a greenhouse. She happily

watered her plants. In another wing, William Holt sat reading about rare African violets.

"Poison Ivy is the happiest-looking person I've ever seen in Arkham," said Commissioner Gordon.

Batman shook his head. "She doesn't care about anything living or breathing besides plant life. In here, no human can bother her, and she can't hurt anyone."

In her cell, Poison Ivy was home. She was happy to stay there forever and live among the flowers.

At least for now...

Fluency Fun

The words in each list below end in the same sounds.
Read the words in a list.
Read them again.
Read them faster.
Try to read all 15 words in one minute.

around	beauty	crawled
found	city	hypnotized
ground	grocery	pulled
pound	Ivy	returned
sound	party	surprised

Look for these words in the story.

special	people	toward
beautiful	human	

Note to Parents:

According to *A Dictionary of Reading and Related Terms*, fluency is "the ability to read smoothly, easily, and readily with freedom from word-recognition problems." Fluency is necessary for good comprehension and enjoyable reading. The activities on this page include a speed drill and a sight-recognition drill. Speed drills build fluency because they help students rapidly recognize common syllables and spelling patterns in words, and they're fun! Sight-recognition drills help students smoothly and accurately recognize words. Practice these activities with your child to help him or her become a fluent reader.

—**Wiley Blevins**
Reading Specialist